To my husband John and
my kids Jesse, Chana and Talya

Parent's Introduction

We Both Read is the first series of books designed to invite parents and children to share the reading of a story by taking turns reading aloud. This "shared reading" innovation, which was developed in conjunction with early reading specialists, invites parents to read the more sophisticated text on the left-hand pages, while children are encouraged to read the right-hand pages, which have been written at one of three early reading levels.

Reading aloud is one of the most important activities parents can share with their child to assist their reading development. However, *We Both Read* goes beyond reading *to* a child and allows parents to share reading *with* a child. *We Both Read* is so powerful and effective because it combines two key elements in learning: "showing" (the parent reads) and "doing" (the child reads). The result is not only faster reading development for the child, but a much more enjoyable and enriching experience for both!

Most of the words used in the child's text should be familiar to them. Others can easily be sounded out. An occasional difficult word will be first introduced in the parent's text, distinguished with **bold lettering**. Pointing out these words, as you read them, will help familiarize them to your child. You may also find it helpful to read the entire book aloud yourself the first time, then invite your child to participate on the second reading. Also note that the parent's text is preceded by a "talking parent" icon: ⬡ ; and the child's text is preceded by a "talking child" icon: ⬡ .

We Both Read books is a fun, easy way to encourage and help your child to read — and a wonderful way to start your child off on a lifetime of reading enjoyment!

We Both Read: The Birthday Ban in Munchkin Land

We Both Read™ is a trademark of Treasure Bay, Inc.

Published by Treasure Bay, Inc.
17 Parkgrove Drive
South San Francisco, CA 94080 USA

PRINTED IN SINGAPORE

Hardcover ISBN 1-891327-19-4
Paperback ISBN 1-891327-20-8

FIRST EDITION

**We Both Read™ Books
Patent Pending**

WE BOTH READ ™

The Birthday Ban in Munchkin Land

By Dev Ross
Illustrated by David Hohn

TREASURE BAY

Once upon a time in the Land of Oz, the Wicked Witch of the East ruled over the Munchkins. She was a frightful ruler who hated everyone, especially children. In fact, she despised children so much that one day, just to see them cry, she decreed that celebrating **birthdays** was a crime!

The Wicked Witch yelled from on high:

"No **birthdays!** No fun!
The good times are done!
Do just as I say!
Or else you will pay!"

Munchkin twins Meezie and Tweeze were terribly upset, for their birthday was on that very day. And now, because of the **Wicked Witch,** there would be no celebration.

"That **Wicked Witch** is bad.

She really makes us mad!

We wish she'd go away!

We wish she'd go today!"

Suddenly the twins heard the tinkling of bells, and a beautiful woman with golden hair appeared before them.

"I am Glinda, the Good Witch of the South," she said. "I have a **wise** old friend who may know how to free the Land of Oz from the Wicked Witch."

"Climb up the hill with me.
Up to a **wise** old Tree.
Old Tree may know the way
to make her go away."

Then Glinda led the twins up the hill to a magnificent oak tree. He was old and gnarled, with two gentle eyes, a round knobby nose and a kind mouth in the middle of his trunk.

Tree gently surrounded the children with his branches and asked, "How can I help you today?"

The twins replied:

"The Witch said no fun!
The good times are done!
Do you know the way
to send her away?"

Wise old Tree pointed to a deep, dark cave. The kind of cave that often houses **bears.**

"The only one who can make the Witch go away is hiding inside that cold, vast cave," said Tree.

Tweeze peered into the dark cave and said:

"I won't go in there.
There might be a **bear!**
I think it's okay
to let the Witch stay!"

"There are no bears," Tree assured the twins as he gently shooed a pesky woodpecker away. "Just a blustery young Windbag."

Seeing how terrified her brother was, Meezie bravely volunteered to call upon Windbag while Tweeze helped Tree **chase** woodpeckers away.

She went to the mouth of the cave and shouted:

"The Witch is so bad.
The Witch makes us mad!
Please **chase** her away.
Please help us today."

Young Windbag stirred and rustled inside the cave. Then he blew out a gust of wind that nearly knocked Meezie off her feet! But Meezie stood her ground.

"Glinda **brought** us to Tree and Tree **brought** us to you! We need your help, Windbag, to make the Witch go away!"

All was silent for a moment—then a voice replied:

"I think you should know
I can't make her go.
I **brought** the Witch here.
I **brought** her! Oh dear!"

Meezie was shocked. "Windbag! Why would you do such a dreadful thing!"

"I didn't mean to," Windbag sniffled, finally showing himself at the mouth of the cave. "I was just showing off how hard I could blow to my friends, Rain and Snow, and I accidentally made a **tornado!**"

"I blew and blew and blew!
A big **tornado** grew!
I'm just a little kid!
I ran away and hid!"

Windbag explained that, as the tornado grew, it reached high into the sky where, by **chance,** the Wicked Witch was flying by (on her way to **France**). Windbag's tornado plucked her right off her broom and plunked her down in the Land of Oz.

With tears in his eyes, Windbag said:

"I made her land here.
Now we live in fear!
It is not by **chance**
she is not in **France!**"

Tweeze, too upset now to be frightened, rushed toward Windbag with angry tears in his eyes. "It's all your fault, Windbag! You ruined our birthday!"

Windbag **listened** to Tweeze's words and felt so terrible that he started to cry again!

But Meezie did *not* cry. Meezie had an idea.

"Let's send the Witch away.
Let's make her go today.
If we are smart we can.
Just **listen** to my plan!"

Meezie quickly laid out her plan to the others. And a short time later, the twins began the first part—a birthday celebration! The children gave each other chocolate birthday pies, then stood on their heads and giggled while wiggling their toes (for that is how Munchkins celebrate their birthdays, you see).

And just as they knew she would, the Witch soon appeared . . .

"No birthdays! No fun!
The good times are done!
You stop this birthday!
Or I'll make you pay!"

The Wicked Witch swooped down on her broom intent on grabbing the twins with her thin, bony fingers, (which was exactly part of the plan)!

Right on cue Windbag blew in. He swirled round and round the Witch until she became so dizzy, she **dropped** right off of her broom—and into a chocolate pie!

Meezie and Tweeze laughed and said:

"We're glad you **dropped** by.
We hope you like pie.
We're glad you could stay
for our birthday today!"

Furious, the Witch chased after them, (which, of course, was also part of the plan).

It was then that Tweeze did something that was *not* in the plan. He turned and stuck out his tongue at the Witch!

The Witch was so shocked that she stopped running, which gave Windbag just enough time to swallow an extra helping of wind before he whirled around her.

While Windbag gulped more air, Tweeze boldly said:

"You have made us mad.

You have made kids sad.

You are going away.

You are going today!"

Windbag had **learned** a **lesson** from his past mistake. He learned that if he swallowed lots of wind then blew really hard, he could create a huge tornado. And that's just what he did. Only now, because of that extra helping of wind he gulped, *this* tornado was even bigger than his first one!

This whirling tornado scooped up the Wicked Witch and carried her high up into the sky.

The Witch shouted down to the twins below:

"Someday I'll make you pay
for treating me this way!
Someday when I return,
a **lesson** you will **learn!**"

But the twins could barely hear the angry Witch, for the twisting tornado was already carrying her far into the distance. Little did they know that it was headed for a strange new place called Kansas.

At last the sky was clear. Everything was **okay.** The Wicked Witch seemed gone for good.

Tweeze was so happy he shouted:

"Look up in the sky!
Look up there so high!
The plan worked **okay!**
The Witch blew away!"

The twins were so excited that they hugged the last remaining gusts of wind from their new friend Windbag, then ran back to tell old Tree all that had happened.

"The wind blew and blew.
The tornado grew!
The Witch blew away.
And away she will stay!"

Indeed, it looked like the Land of Oz was free of the Wicked Witch at last.

But then something extraordinary happened. The big, scary tornado carrying the Witch suddenly reappeared! It had returned from its trip to that strange place called Kansas—and now it was carrying a house!

Meezie could hardly believe her eyes!

"The tornado is back.
It looks scary and black!
And a house is inside
Do you think we should hide?"

Then, just as suddenly as it had returned, the spinning, whirling, terrible tornado fizzled out. And as it fizzled, everything it had carried dropped down to the ground. The Wicked Witch fell first. Then the house fell right on top of her.

When the Munchkins of Oz saw this, they cried out in glee:

"The house fell from the sky.

It fell from way up high.

The Wicked Witch is dead.

The house fell on her head!"

There was a rattle and creak as the battered front door of the small house opened and a sweet little girl with long brown braids peeked out.

"Hello," said the girl, "my name is **Dorothy.**"

It was Dororthy's house that had flattened the Witch and the Munchkins all cheered her and sang.

"**Dorothy's** house fell down.
It fell down to the ground.
The Wicked Witch is done.
Now we can all have fun!"

Tweeze was disappointed that Dorothy was getting all the credit for ridding Oz of the Wicked Witch. After all, he and Meezie and Windbag had created the tornado in the first place!

But Meezie didn't mind at all. She was just happy to have this **perfect** day on which to celebrate their birthday.

She took her brother's hands in hers and sang:

"Today is our birthday
Our birthday is today!
Happy, happy birthday!
What a **perfect** day!"

If you liked
The Birthday Ban in Munchkin Land, **here are two other** *We Both Read*™ **Books you are sure to enjoy!**

The classic tale of two very hungry children who are lost in the woods. Hansel and Gretel find a fantastic gingerbread house, but the owner is a very wicked witch. Featuring the beautifully stylized and very whimsical art of Tim Barnes, this childhood favorite will be more exciting than ever with the shared reading of We Both Read.

This lively retelling of the classic story is filled with humor and excitement. Much to his mother's dismay, Jack trades their only cow for five beans. But from these beans grows a magic beanstalk, which Jack climbs up to confront a fearsome giant. Jack must outwit and outrun the giant to reclaim his family's golden treasures!